Blu

Jared Cade is the Amazon number one bestselling author of *Agatha Christie and the Eleven Missing Days*. He is a former tour guide for a bespoke luxury travel company, escorting parties around Agatha Christie's home, Greenway, which is open to the public courtesy of the National Trust. During an appearance on the British television quiz *The $64,000 Question*, he won the top prize on his specialist subject of Agatha Christie's novels. Jared Cade is the creator of the Lyle Revel and Hermione Bradbury mysteries. He is also a member of the Crime Writers' Association and Society of Authors. Readers can connect with Jared Cade on Facebook.

Also by Jared Cade

Jared Cade

Blue Mountains Tragedy

SCARAB BOOKS

Published by Scarab Books
18 Wandsworth Road
London SW8 2JB

ISBN 9798874461317

Cover Design by GermanCreative

Blue Mountains Tragedy

As Saffron drove her BMW through the rain-lashed night towards Katoomba Police Station, she was forced to confront her ambivalent feelings for her murdered friend. Ailsa Kennedy had been brimming with happiness a short while ago but now she was dead on the living-room floor of her home, bereft of all thoughts and emotions.

Shock and horror seared through every fibre of Saffron's being. The memory of Ailsa's laughter grated on her nerves like a file on glass. If the teenage Ailsa hadn't been laughing helplessly as Saffron snagged her tongue on her braces, then the latter-day Ailsa of forty – hair dyed defiantly as black as a raven's wing – had been just as amused at Saffron's recent dismay in discovering that her new swimsuit had become transparent when wet.

After retiring from the international ballet circuit two years ago, Ailsa had moved to the Blue Mountains and set up her own dancing school which she had sold six months later following her marriage to Preston Kennedy. As a wealthy, award-winning composer of some of Australia's best known and best loved film and television scores, Preston had been targeted over the years by several females hoping to become his wife, but no one had been successful until Ailsa had come along and beguiled him with her charms.

On the journey to the Blue Mountains earlier that evening, Saffron's relief in leaving behind Sydney's rat race had been undermined by the bad weather. There was nothing like driving to the Blue Mountains on a clear summer's day. Owing to the densely populated oil-bearing Eucalyptus trees, the atmosphere was always filled with finely dispersed droplets of oil, dust particles and water vapour that omitted a blue haze over the mountains.

On Saffron's arrival, Ailsa had greeted her in a silver lamé dress and a jangling of bracelets.

'You look tired from your trip,' she said, taking her upstairs to the guest bedroom. *'Why don't you have a scented bath? It will help you to relax and unwind. Preston can get the rest of your luggage out of the car when he gets home.'*

Saffron struggled to keep the disappointment out of her voice. *'Where is he?'*

'Don't tell me you've forgotten Preston plays squash every Monday night at the Katoomba Sports Centre,' said Ailsa, staring at her in surprise. *'He won't be back for another couple of hours. Once he gets home, he's expecting Broderick Tanner to come by with some papers.'*

Broderick Tanner owned his own successful record label and had been Preston Kennedy's manager for years.

'He could have chosen a better night,'

3

remarked Saffron, as a loud crack of thunder set her nerves on edge.

Ailsa shrugged indifferently. *'Apparently there are discrepancies in Preston's latest royalty statement. Come downstairs for a gin and tonic when you're ready. We'll have some nibbles with our drinks to ward off the hunger pangs while we wait for the men to get here. Once they've finished talking business, we'll have scrambled eggs and smoked salmon for supper –'*

Preston – out playing squash? Saffron had expected him to be there to greet her. The prescribed soak in the bath had taken the edge off her disappointment. There had been consolation in knowing that she had brought Preston and Ailsa together.

Shortly after her engagement, Ailsa had confided to Saffron, *'Preston and I couldn't be happier. I need a man to challenge me and he's the first man I'm able to respect for it. It still amazes me that you used the same horse-riding stables as Preston for a year without telling me about him...'*

If the thought had crossed Saffron's mind

prior to the couple's marriage that Preston Kennedy was far too good for Ailsa, the idea had not taken root until earlier that night when she had emerged on the staircase landing overlooking the front hall. That was when she had heard Ailsa's voice coming from the living-room. Her usual languid tones had been hard and clipped.

'Can't you just accept I'm a married woman and leave it at that? Divorcing my husband for you would lead to all sorts of complications that are best avoided for everyone's sake.'

Saffron paused on the landing, intent on hearing the worst.

'Honestly, you're as bad as any other man I've known.' Ailsa's laugh turned brittle. *'Totally indifferent to anyone else's feelings apart from your own. Darling, how many times do I have to tell you? My being married to another man doesn't change my feelings for you –?'*

Saffron hated recalling the sound of the pistol shot that had followed…

'What's going on?' she cried. *'Who's*

there?'

She heard footsteps moving across the pine floorboards of the living-room in the direction of the archway. It was as if the killer had heard her outburst although the words had died a silent death before reaching her lips.

For reasons Saffron didn't understand, the footsteps veered further back into the living-room. The sound of overturning furniture reached her – and then a cool draught of air swept out of the living-room into the front hall and invaded the staircase landing...

Below her in the front hall, the grandfather clock softly chimed eight o'clock. Each chime sounded like a death knell for Ailsa.

Saffron heard the killer's car taking off from in front of the house. The paralysis of fear that had frozen her to the landing released its hold. By the time she raced downstairs and looked out of the front window, all she could see was the blackness of the night and her own horrified reflection staring back at her...

Ailsa was lying sprawled on the living-room rug, beyond help, looking like a bird with a broken wing. The sight of her eyes gazing into eternity sent a shudder through Saffron.

The French windows leading onto the side terrace were open and the curtains were billowing in the wind and rain. The killer had ripped the phone cord out of the wall socket and cut it in half to prevent anyone from calling the police. Saffron had been unable to contact them on her mobile because the battery was flat...

Now, as the windscreen wipers squelched back and forth in front of her, Saffron glanced at the speedometer. The hand on the dial was pushing 80. Katoomba Police Station was four miles away, but she dared not drive any faster in the downpour. The road was far too treacherous...

Uppermost in her mind, like a squirrel chasing its own tail, ran the same thought on auto-repeat, *The police are going to want to know who killed Ailsa...*

Saffron was determined to report her friend's murder to the police and assist them in their investigation, but how could she when she didn't know the identity of Ailsa's jilted lover? Owing to her failure to see his face before he fled from the scene of the crime, anger and self-recrimination lanced through her.

If only she hadn't been so tired earlier in the night and had questioned Ailsa about her latest affair. There had to be a clue to the killer's identity in her friend's past that would provide her with the necessary flash of inspiration to strip away his mask of anonymity.

Earlier in the week, Saffron had received an email from Ailsa in which she had boasted, *'I'm in seventh heaven after going for a roll in the hay with one of the Blue Mountains' most handsome studs. I'll tell you all about it when we get some time alone. Come up on Monday as planned – you're welcome to stay the entire week if you like.'*

Saffron stifled a sob. The phrase 'a roll in the hay' suggested Ailsa's lover had been her riding instructor. Beau Constantine ran his widowed mother's horse-riding stables for her. His darkly handsome looks were overlaid with a great deal of boyish charm. He was young, too, which is how Ailsa liked her men. Yet

Saffron was reluctant to believe that Beau Constantine was the killer. The look of vulnerability in his calf-brown eyes, along with his gentle manner, suggested to her that he wasn't the aggressive type. On the other hand, suppose he was more repressed than he outwardly appeared and liable to explode into violence when he didn't get his own way? If only she could be sure...

What if Ailsa's jilted lover was Broderick Tanner? A distinguished silver-haired man with a taste for the finer things in life, Broderick Tanner was Preston's business manager and owned his own private horse-riding stables. There had apparently been no one special in Broderick Tanner's life for years. It seemed his first wife had drowned, his second had died in a car crash and his third had died of a drug overdose. Ailsa had always spoken dismissively of him – and with good reason. Prior to meeting Preston, she had tried to seduce Broderick Tanner and had been shocked to discover he was impervious to her charms. It wasn't altogether surprising since he was a confirmed widower of sixty-five whose heart had been broken too many times in love. Who then had killed Ailsa?

David Foster...

The name dropped unexpectedly into Saffron's mind. She momentarily relaxed her grip on the steering wheel and veered too far to the left of the road before she regained control of the BMW. In addition to being ten years younger than Ailsa, he was also extremely good-looking. Did being a doctor prevent him from also being a murderer?

'David Foster...' The memory of Ailsa's voice came to Saffron along with her friend's enigmatic smile. *'Now there's a catch – if only a woman has what it takes...'*

The more Saffron thought about it the more convinced she became that Ailsa had been having an affair with him...

On coming to the Blue Mountains over a year ago, Dr. Foster had revitalized the running of the Constantine Community Hospital. One day Ailsa had been rushed to hospital suffering from abdominal cramps. Dr. Foster had saved her life by removing her appendix before it ruptured. After being released from hospital a grateful Ailsa had invited him to join her and Preston for afternoon tea at their home which is how Saffron had met the physician.

Saffron had found David Foster arrogant and self-opinionated. To make matters worse, she had got into an argument with him over the benefits of acupuncture. The Englishman's posh voice had put Preston's Australian twang in the shade. Tensions had flared further when David Foster had mentioned he and Ailsa had met years ago in London while she was performing as a ballerina on the European dance circuit.

Preston had got up abruptly from the table and announced he was going to play squash. He had later told Saffron, *'The great thing about playing squash is that you can imagine the ball is the head of anyone who's annoying you.'*

Although Ailsa had mentioned once or twice that Preston had a violent temper, Saffron had never seen any sign of it. She was aware Ailsa had been fond of dramatizing herself and had never let the truth get in the way of a good story.

A sudden thought shook Saffron. *If I don't tell the police what happened tonight, they could make the mistake of thinking Preston killed Ailsa...*

She gritted her teeth as a virulent squall of rain pelted the windscreen. Katoomba Police Station seemed an eternity away. Matters weren't helped by visibility growing poorer by the second. The windscreen wipers were struggling to cope with the onslaught. The BMW skidded on some mud that had been washed onto the road by the deluge...

Everything took place after that in a slow motion time warp. The way the car went into a tailspin – the way the white trunk of a Eucalyptus tree loomed up in front of the windscreen....

Saffron's last conscious thought was, *If I'd made my presence known on the stairs earlier tonight David Foster wouldn't have killed Ailsa...*

Saffron regained consciousness slowly. A dreamlike shadow play of shapes and sounds was going on about her. She prayed for the oblivion of sleep, and the comforting, steadfast presence of Preston Kennedy. Then she felt the gentle squeeze of his hand and knew this was the best part of her dream.

'Take it easy.' Preston's masculine voice came to her as if from the depths and his handsome, reassuring, bullock-like features swam in and out of focus before her eyes. 'You're going to be fine.'

'*No, I'm not,*' she wanted to tell him and burst into hysterical sobs. Her body ached and throbbed all over.

A rumble of thunder shook the night and she heard rain splashing against the window of her hospital room.

'You've been in an accident,' explained Preston gently.

Saffron tried to speak but her sobs were too intense. She hoped he would go on holding her hand and that the dream would last forever.

'Your car ran off the road a few miles from

the house,' he added. 'A passing motorist found you. Now I know you're going to be okay, I'll go home and bring Ailsa back to see you. I've tried phoning her to let her know what's happened, but for some reason she isn't picking up.'

Without knowing why, Saffron suddenly hated Ailsa more than she had ever hated anyone. Animal cries rose up in her throat, drowning out the rest of the dream. Suddenly she was drifting along, safe and secure...

She woke with a start to find David Foster standing at the foot of the bed. The lean, craggy-faced physician's hair was wet, and she shivered involuntarily. As a child she had been terrified of people when their hair was wet. She struggled to concentrate on what he was saying.

'You'll be walking out of here in a few days' time with a clean bill of health. Unless you do something foolish you should live to a ripe old age.'

'*Ailsa...*'

The name escaped Saffron's lips in a hoarse whisper. It all came flooding back. The scene she had overheard on the stairs...the awful sound of the shot...the discovery of Ailsa's body on the living-room rug...

'Your friend Preston Kennedy was here half an hour ago,' continued Dr. Foster. 'Someone at the Katoomba Sports Centre heard about your accident and told him about it.'

So, it hadn't been a dream... Preston had really been at her bedside when she had needed him most... How could she have let him leave her without telling him what had happened to Ailsa...?

Saffron was shaking with suppressed hysteria. *'You can't let him find her like that. She's dead – dead...'*

'What on earth –?'

'I was there on the stairs when she was shot. I was coming down the road for help when my car ran into some sludge and went into a tailspin ...'

Her gaze locked with David Foster's. His eyes gleamed with the fierce determination of a ruthless egotist. There was something unpredictable about him that was unnerving –

15

dangerous even...

'You've got to let me speak to the police...' Saffron fought against her overwhelming suspicions of him. 'If anything were to happen to me, they might think Ailsa was killed by her husband...'

Dr. Foster spoke to her as if he were humouring a child. 'Try to relax and get some rest. We'll talk again later...'

The corners of his mouth were upturned in a faint smile as he returned an empty hypodermic syringe to its case and slipped it into his pocket. Saffron felt a sharp inward tug, like a violent undertow. He must have given her something just before she regained consciousness to silence her forever...

A terrifying wave of darkness dragged Saffron down into its depths... Disturbed, fragmented images came and went. All of them to do with Ailsa – if only she could figure out what they meant... It was vitally important for her to decipher them although she didn't understand the how or why of it...

Presently, a series of burning candles rose before her eyes... Unless she spoke out to save

Preston, he would be mourning Ailsa from behind prison bars for a murder he had not committed. She was determined not to let David Foster get away with killing Ailsa...

'How long have I been here?'

This was the first question Saffron asked the Aboriginal nurse on waking up. The storm had passed and a band of bright sunlight streamed across her bed. A symphony of different bird songs, interspersed with a kookaburra's loud cackle of 'koo-koo-koo-koo-koo-kaa-kaa-kaa', reached Saffron's ears. The window of her hospital room overlooked an expanse of Eucalyptus bushland and she glimpsed the flash of an exotic Rainbow Lorikeet flying past.

'You were brought here three days ago,' replied the nurse. 'You're going to be fine.'

The tension ebbed from Saffron's body. She was alive, thank God, alive... David Foster couldn't have been trying to kill her. He wasn't Ailsa's jilted lover, after all...

As the nurse left the room, Dr. Foster appeared in the doorway and gazed appraisingly at his patient.

'Ah – you're finally awake,' he said. 'How are you feeling today?'

'Much stronger,' lied Saffron, disliking his friendly manner. 'Is it true I've been totally out of it for three days?'

'The last time we spoke you were completely delirious. I couldn't understand what you were saying.'

Saffron stared at him in shock.

Liar, liar, liar – he had deliberately ignored her pleas...

'Have you any recollections of what happened before your accident?'

Saffron was determined not to fall into any further traps he set for her. 'I – I was planning to spend a week with my friends here in the Blue Mountains,' she faltered.

Dr. Foster's voice took on a faint edge. 'Your friend Ailsa Kennedy has been murdered...'

'Murdered?' she repeated, trying to look surprised.

'The police aren't convinced that it was the work of a burglar. They suspect Preston killed her after getting home that night.'

So, that was why Dr. Foster had ignored her pleas for help... He had wanted Preston to go home and discover Ailsa's body. It was a staple diet of television crime dramas that the first person the police always suspected was the individual who found the body...

'Why should he want to kill Ailsa?' she croaked.

'Ailsa was an attractive woman,' said Dr. Foster bluntly. 'Preston has always been possessive. He's known to have a violent temper.'

'N–no, I refuse to believe he killed Ailsa.'

Dr. Foster's footsteps rang out sharply as he rounded the bed. 'Can you think of anyone who would want to harm her?'

Saffron shuddered. The sound of his footsteps reminded her of the footsteps she had heard in the living-room after the murder...

'Ailsa's flamboyant style offended the Blue Mountains' social elite,' she stammered. 'Perhaps one of them killed her –'

'I find that most unlikely.' Dr. Foster halted in his tracks with a tight smile on his lips.

'You've clearly had a shock. I'll get you a cup of tea and a slice of toast to ward off your hunger pangs until lunch is served –'

Saffron stiffened. Although the Constantine Community Hospital was a small sixty-bed establishment, doctors in her experience always delegated the menial tasks to nurses. Why was he pretending to be so nice to her?

'But you must be busy,' she protested. 'Surely one of the nurses –'

'It's no trouble,' he insisted firmly.

On Dr. Foster's return, Saffron was feeling lightheaded with hunger. She did not hesitate to eat the toast he put before her. The tea was another matter. Dr. Foster was clearly going to stay until she finished it. She took a tentative sip. It tasted unnaturally sweet. Surely he couldn't have expected her to like her tea this sweet unless –

After a sidelong glance at Saffron, the physician stepped outside into the corridor to confer with the Aboriginal nurse. Saffron heard their whispered exchange, but she was unable to work out what they were saying. There were no pot plants in the room. Saffron poured the tea into the bedside drawer. She had barely closed it before Dr. Foster returned.

'Finished already?' Dr. Foster glanced at the empty cup and nodded as if strangely satisfied. 'I'll look in on you later...'

The firmness with which he took the cup from Saffron unnerved her. She watched him leave the room and listened to his footsteps receding down the corridor. As the nurse re-entered the room and fluffed up her pillows, Saffron felt her courage return.

'Would you mind taking me to the chapel?' she asked. 'I want to say a prayer for my friend Ailsa.'

'Of course...'

On the way there, Saffron scanned the corridor for a phone but she was unable to see one. The nurse left her sitting alone on a pew with a promise to return and take her back to her room in around twenty minutes' time. The only natural light in the chapel came from a small circular stained glass window. Anyone passing outside in the corridor would have been hard-pressed to notice Saffron if they had glanced into the gloomy interior. She was lost in her own thoughts when voices reached her presently from outside in the corridor.

'Beau, what are you doing here?' asked Pearl Constantine. 'Why is your arm in a sling?'

She was a rich, dictatorial matriarch who had buried her only husband some years ago after bearing him seven sons who now danced to her tune by running her vineyards and horse-riding stables for her. The result of having so many sons had left her looking thin and gaunt. There was nothing soft about Pearl Constantine's appearance apart from her blue-rinsed perm which she wore around her head like a helmet. Widowhood suited her combative personality and the considerable wealth and power she had accumulated meant she ruled the Blue Mountains' social hierarchy with a fist of iron.

Despite being darkly handsome and over six foot tall, Pearl Constantine's youngest son Beau was devoid of a strong intellect and lacked confidence. He stood before his mother looking as servile as a child.

'Rusty threw me off while I was out riding this morning,' he mumbled.

Pearl Constantine's brow furrowed. 'He's normally such a placid horse.'

'Something must have spooked him. The fall bruised my shoulder and arm. I'll be all right in a few days.'

'Has anyone spoken to you about the night of the murder?' demanded Pearl Constantine.

Beau's reply was quiet and submissive. 'No, mother.'

'Remember – if anyone asks you were at home playing poker with me and your brothers.'

'But I went for a drive by myself out to Govetts Leap,' protested Beau. 'I liked the way the rain drummed down on the windscreen. It was so quiet and peaceful without a single soul in the world to intrude on my thoughts –'

Pearl Constantine cut her son off. 'You were at home all night with your brothers and me, is that understood? And another thing. You're to keep your mouth shut on the subject of Preston Kennedy's wife.'

'I swear there was nothing between us.'

'Don't lie to me, Beau.' Pearl Constantine's voice was as taut as the crack of a whip. 'Your brother Leroy has told me everything. A week ago, he visited the riding school. He saw you making love to that tramp – in the stables of all places!'

Beau lowered his head. 'She was a beautiful woman, but I –'

'That's enough, Beau. I don't want to hear another word. Now go home and keep your mouth shut. There's a meeting of the hospital board of directors to discuss the funding for the new wing. I mustn't be late for it –'

The mother and son moved off down the corridor.

Saffron's thoughts were reeling. Why had Pearl Constantine concocted an alibi for her son Beau *unless she knew he was guilty of Ailsa's murder...?*

As Saffron rose to her feet, she saw a discarded copy of that morning's *Blue Mountains Advertiser* lying near her on the pew. Someone must have visited the chapel and forgotten to take it away with them. The front-page headline turned her stomach.

COMPOSER DENIES KILLING WIFE

After reading that the inquest into Ailsa's death was scheduled to take place at ten o'clock that morning at the Katoomba Coroner's Court, Saffron hurried back to her room. Thankfully the clothes she had been wearing on the night of the car accident were hanging up in the wardrobe. She dressed quickly and then went in search of a phone. She needed to summon a taxi to take her to the inquest. Her furtive quest took her to a deserted office where the clock on the wall revealed it was already ten-forty-five.

As Saffron reached for the phone, she saw the nameplate on the desk: *Dr. David Foster.* A shiver ran through her body. Although she was convinced Beau Constantine had killed Ailsa, she still couldn't bring herself to trust David Foster. He was keeping something back from her – she felt certain of it...

The window of Dr. Foster's office

overlooked the front driveway of the hospital. She saw a taxi pull up and disgorge an elderly couple. Replacing the receiver, she hurried outside and instructed the driver to take her to the Katoomba Coroner's Court.

Smooth, urbane and impeccably dressed in a tie and suit, Broderick Tanner was testifying in the witness box. He broke off as Saffron entered the court. His thatch of silver-grey hair crowned a distinguished head with a lantern jaw. Quickly recovering his composure, he turned to the coroner and spoke in a crisp voice.

'That's Saffron Duvall – the retired international tennis champion. She was driving to the Kennedys' house on the night of the murder when her car came off the road. She's been in hospital ever since –'

The coroner, a fussy birdlike man, looked up with keen intelligence.

'I was there in the house when Ailsa was murdered,' blurted Saffron. 'I was driving down the road to get help when I lost control of my car. I know what happened –'

Once Broderick Tanner had finished testifying, the coroner invited Saffron to take her place in the witness box. After being sworn in, she told the court everything she could about the night of the murder.

'After the long drive from Sydney, I was feeling worn out when I arrived at the Kennedys' house,' she explained. 'Ailsa took me upstairs to my room and urged me to have a scented bath. After I got dressed again it was almost eight o'clock. I got as far as the staircase landing when I overheard Ailsa talking to her lover in the living-room. They had obviously been arguing. She was trying to reassure him that being a married woman didn't change the way she felt towards him. He clearly didn't believe her – and that's when he shot her dead...'

'Did Mrs. Kennedy ever confide to you the name of the man she was having an affair with?' asked the coroner.

Saffron shook her head. 'Ailsa recently sent me an email saying she had taken a roll in the hay with one of the Blue Mountains' most handsome studs. Although she didn't mention his name, it was obvious she was referring to her riding instructor Beau Constantine –'

The coroner interrupted her. 'Your suspicions are entirely unfounded. I have a deposition here from Mrs. Constantine confirming her son was at home with his family on the night of the murder.'

'That can't be right,' insisted Saffron. 'Beau Constantine told his mother that he went for a drive to the lookout at Govetts Leap. He claimed there had been no one around to intrude on his thoughts.'

The coroner frowned. 'Are you sure he was referring to the night of Monday 2 April?'

'Yes.'

'When did you hear Beau Constantine telling his mother this?'

'Earlier this morning. They were talking to each other in the corridor of the Constantine Community Hospital. I was in the chapel and overheard every word they said to each other. Pearl Constantine was furious with Beau for insisting he went to Govetts Leap on the night of the murder. She ordered him to say he had been at home with her and his brothers.'

'Are you certain the voices belonged to Mrs. Constantine and her son Beau?'

Saffron nodded. 'I could see them both clearly through the chapel doorway. When Beau denied having an affair with Ailsa, Pearl Constantine told him that another of her sons Leroy had visited the riding school a week before the murder and had seen Beau making love to Ailsa in the stables –'

The coroner nodded succinctly as if satisfied with her testimony and went on making detailed notes. A short while later, he put down his pen and addressed the court.

'The sequence of events on the night of the murder is much clearer thanks to Miss Duvall's testimony. Various witnesses have confirmed Preston Kennedy was at the Katoomba Sports Centre playing squash between seven-thirty and nine o'clock. Mrs. Kennedy was shot in the living-room of their home at eight o'clock. Whoever came to the house that night was evidently not aware that Miss Duvall was staying there as a guest. After shooting Mrs. Kennedy, the killer drove away in an unidentified vehicle which indicates he must live some distance away. This inquest is adjourned pending further police inquiries –'

As the proceedings came to an end, an excited babble of voices broke out in the public gallery. The din reminded Saffron of a swarm of bees buzzing over a carcass. There appeared to be very little doubt in any one's mind as she and Preston left the court that Beau Constantine was now the number one suspect in the case.

Saffron and Preston eluded the press by accompanying Broderick Tanner in his Land Rover to his home which was situated several miles further up the road from the Kennedy property. The businessman owned a two-million-dollar rural estate called Inglewood complete with manicured lawns, a private lake and horse-riding stables. Despite the strain and grief Preston was under, he was holding up better than Saffron had expected and she felt relieved for his sake.

On the third day of their stay, Saffron went for a walk through the Eucalyptus bushland bordering the property. The fresh air and exercise did her the world of good. A man startled her by stepping out from behind a tree. She recognized him at once. It was Leroy Constantine. He was an older, lankier version of his brother with hooded eyelids like a lizard's.

'That was quite a stunt you pulled at the inquest!' he jeered. 'You had no right to implicate Beau in that woman's murder. My family never forgets a slight or forgives anyone who injures them.'

'Let go of me,' said Saffron coldly.

She wrenched her wrist free from Leroy Constantine's grasp. The intense sexual magnetism emanating from him was extra-ordinary. It occurred to her that he must have seduced lots of females with those piercing blue eyes.

'You can run but you can't hide,' he called after her.

Saffron was breathing hard when she got back to Inglewood. Broderick was sitting opposite Preston in the living-room discussing the outstanding balance on the latter's royalty statement.

'Axel Productions has gone bankrupt,' Broderick was saying with an air of professional regret. 'You're one of several creditors. I doubt if we'll ever see the money they owe you –'

Saffron immediately told them about her disturbing encounter with Leroy Constantine.

'It's too bad you didn't catch him walking on my property,' growled Broderick. 'I could have had him arrested for trespassing.'

Preston put his arm protectively around Saffron and she felt a shiver of sexual excitement that had lain dormant for too long.

'Thank goodness you're all right,' he said gently. 'I want you to stay away from the Constantines. They're as venomous as a pit of rattlesnakes...'

Later that night, while they were having dinner, a rock was hurtled through the dining-room window. There was no message attached to it and they had no way of knowing who the culprit was. Saffron was convinced Leroy Constantine was responsible...

Shortly after this, Saffron returned to Sydney. Although she had retired from playing international tennis, she was kept busy coaching her clients.

Over the next six months, she visited the Blue Mountains and spent each weekend with Preston at the home he had once shared with Ailsa. Saffron was aware of his growing emotional dependency on her and she was determined to do all that she could to help him recover from the trauma of Ailsa's murder. They soon became lovers and rode occasionally in the grounds of Broderick Tanner's property.

One day Preston took Saffron by the hand and said simply, 'Marry me...'

Although she had been expecting him to broach the subject of marriage for some time, his proposal still brought tears to her eyes.

'Preston, there's nothing I'd like more than to marry you and become your wife,' she said shakily. 'But I'm not sure this terrible guilt I'm feeling will ever go away –'

'You've got to stop blaming yourself for Ailsa's death,' insisted Preston. 'What if you had got to the window sooner and seen the killer driving off down the road? It was too late by then to save her. We've got to be patient. Beau Constantine will eventually get his comeuppance...'

After returning the horses to the stables, they entered Broderick Tanner's house to find him on the phone. He was looking unusually grim as he hung up.

'It's happened,' he began.

'What are you talking about?' asked Preston.

'Beau Constantine is dead,' said Broderick. 'The strain of being hounded by the police and living under the shadow of suspicion has proved too much.'

'Are you saying he's taken the easy way out?' demanded Preston.

Broderick nodded. 'I told you he was weak and wouldn't be able to cope with being ostracized publicly. I'm surprised he didn't take the coward's way out before now. His car was found at Govetts Leap in the early hours of this morning. The emergency services have retrieved his body from the foot of the cliff.'

Saffron was shocked by the news of Beau Constantine's suicide. The unexpected turn of events was sure to result in considerable gossip and speculation amongst the locals.

'The police ought to have arrested Beau before now,' said Preston, his voice hardening with anger. 'Thanks to their inept handling of the case we're never going to see him convicted of Ailsa's murder in a court of law.'

'Some things can't be helped,' said Saffron, squeezing his hand comfortingly. 'Now that Beau Constantine is dead let's be thankful he's no longer in a position to harm anyone else...'

On the drive back to Preston's house Saffron wondered if it was as simple as that. Memory took her back to the morning in the hospital chapel when she had overheard Pearl Constantine confronting her son in the corridor.

'Don't lie to me, Beau. Your brother Leroy has told me everything. A week ago, he visited the riding school. He saw you making love to that tramp – in the stables of all places!'

Rather than admit his guilt, Beau had simply hung his head and said, *'She was a beautiful woman, but I –'*

Before he could finish speaking, Pearl Constantine had ordered him to go home. At the time Saffron had assumed Beau was about to admit to having an affair with Ailsa. Suppose he had really been going to say something like, *'But I never made love to Ailsa. Leroy made that up to cover his tracks because he slept with her and didn't want you to find out'?*

Saffron's thoughts chilled her. What if Leroy had murdered Ailsa and faked his younger brother's suicide so everyone would *assume* a guilty conscience had prompted Beau to kill himself? Rather than upset Preston, Saffron kept her suspicions to herself.

A fortnight before Saffron and Preston were due to exchange their vows, Broderick Tanner surprised them by announcing he was unable to attend their wedding due to an important business trip. Saffron was secretly relieved. Preston relied on him too much and was naïve when it came to money matters. She had never rid herself of the suspicion that Broderick Tanner might be embezzling him. It was entirely possible Axel Productions had paid Broderick Tanner the money they owed Preston before its board of directors had filed for bankruptcy.

Saffron recalled at least two occasions in the past when she had overheard Ailsa telling Preston, *'Broderick Tanner isn't getting any younger. He deserves to retire. You really ought to consider getting a new business manager.'* Was it possible Ailsa had suspected Preston was being embezzled by Broderick Tanner and had confronted the entrepreneur before she died...?

After they were married, Saffron was determined to keep a watchful eye on Preston's finances for him – and, if possible, persuade him to hire someone else to organize his business affairs.

A fierce storm raged over the Blue Mountains on the night before the wedding. Saffron woke from a dreamless sleep. In her drowsy state, she thought she could hear voices reaching her from downstairs in the living-room where Ailsa had been murdered...

The impression faded and she thought to herself, *I must be dreaming.*

'Preston...'

Unnerved by the darkness and the fury of the storm, Saffron found herself reaching out to him. He stirred next to her, his eyelids heavy with sleep.

'Did you say something?' he mumbled.

'It's raining,' she whispered. 'We've left the car windows open. If we don't do anything the sheepskin seat covers will be ruined.'

There was a brief sound of fumbling from Preston's side of the bed and then the bedside light snapped on. Saffron closed her eyes against the sharp glare.

'Go back to sleep,' he urged her gently. 'I won't be long...'

Saffron heard Preston hurrying downstairs followed by the sound of the front door opening and shutting. She must have dozed off because when she woke the lamp was still on and Preston's side of the bed was empty...

She shuddered as she recalled the day

Leroy Constantine had told her, *'My family never forgets a slight or forgives anyone who injures them...'*

A sudden overwhelming desire to make sure Preston was all right prompted Saffron to pull on her satin dressing-gown and leave the bedroom. She was more convinced than ever that Leroy Constantine had hurtled the rock through Inglewood's dining-room window. Suppose he and the rest of his family were planning to wreck her wedding to Preston...?

Saffron's slippered-feet made no sound as she came downstairs. She glanced through the archway into the dimly lit living-room and saw Preston standing with his back to her as he leaned over the antique cedar desk. It had warped slightly on the night of the murder because of the amount of rain that had come in through the open French windows. Saffron heard a sharp jolting sound coming from the desk and wondered what had caused it.

Suddenly, Saffron's attention was drawn by a faint tinkering noise – and she shrank back into the shadows of the front hall. The noise came from somewhere upstairs. Preston must have heard it, too. She saw his silhouette as he came out of the living-room. He walked slowly upstairs – evidently unaware of her presence.

Saffron's heart rate increased as she walked over to the desk. The origin of the unusual sound had been a secret drawer sliding open. Unconsciously holding her breath, she looked inside the drawer and saw a Luger semi-automatic pistol.

So, Preston was aware of Leroy Constantine's vendetta and was prepared for any eventuality. She heard another unident-ified noise and stiffened. Perhaps it was the house settling. On the other hand, suppose Leroy Constantine had broken into an upstairs room and had come to exact a terrifying revenge on her and Preston because her testimony at the inquest had implicated his brother Beau in Ailsa's murder...

Saffron took the pistol from the drawer and came upstairs. The tinkering noise was coming from the spare room. The door was ajar and she pushed it open. A baby's pull cord music box was playing on the chest of drawers. Preston was staring at it. He was standing under the naked light bulb. Only it wasn't Preston. The Preston she knew and loved had never had wet hair. The wet hair phobia of her childhood came rushing back.

Something Preston had once said returned to taunt her: *'You've got to stop blaming yourself for Ailsa's death. What if you had got to the window sooner and seen the killer driving off down the road? It was too late by then to save her...'*

It occurred to Saffron that the killer might just as easily have driven off up the road. How could Preston have known the killer had driven off *down* the road – unless...

'You killed her,' she blurted.

Preston swung round to face her. 'Ailsa didn't tell me she had invited you to stay with us,' he said in a hoarse voice. 'If I'd known you were upstairs, I would never have returned to the house for my squash racket and shot her. I thought I could be mature and handle the truth... Ailsa and David Foster were married years ago in London. Ailsa insisted his decision to come and live here in the Blue Mountains was a coincidence – nothing more.

Apparently, she was convinced he had died in a train crash on the outskirts of London a couple of years into the marriage. His name was listed in the newspapers as one of the dead. But when you think about it David Foster is a common enough name to see in an obituary column. I believed Ailsa when she said she had no idea she was committing bigamy when she married me. In my own way' – Preston's voice trembled – 'I was as vain as Ailsa. I didn't want to believe she had married me for my money. She refused to give me a child and that's when I knew she had lied to me about everything. I knew there had been other men in her life. Somehow it didn't matter – until David Foster entered her life again. She couldn't see he was like the rest of the men she'd slept with and still only wanted one thing.'

'Stop it!' Saffron spoke impassionedly. 'I don't want to hear another word! Thinking about Ailsa isn't going to help either of us. We've got the rest of our lives to look forward to together –'

'It's too late –' insisted Preston.

'Oh, don't be ridiculous!' said Saffron, staring at him in disbelief. 'If you had any sense, you would have got rid of the gun before now.'

'The desk drawer wouldn't open. The rain warped it on the night Ailsa died. What was I supposed to do?'

Saffron's mind was racing. 'How did you fake your alibi? Everyone swears you were at the Katoomba Sports Centre between seven-thirty and nine o'clock.'

'Ailsa wasn't murdered at eight o'clock –'

'But I heard the grandfather clock in the hall chiming eight o'clock.'

'She died at seven o'clock. After visiting you at the hospital, I came home and realized I'd forgotten to put the clocks back one hour the previous night to herald the end of daylight saving. After rectifying the matter, I rang the police on my mobile and played the part of the grieving husband who was horrified to discover his wife had been killed by an intruder.'

'What about Beau Constantine?'

'I didn't kill him if that's what you're

thinking. If he hadn't let Ailsa seduce him in the stables, he'd still be alive today. Being a spineless wonder, he threw himself off Govetts Leap because he couldn't stand the pressure of being suspected of her murder.'

'You've got to pull yourself together and put the past behind you,' said Saffron impatiently. 'We're getting married in several hours' time. The future is all that matters –'

'We're to forget Ailsa – just like that?' mused Preston. 'Is that it?'

Saffron felt as if chards of glass had entered her dream.

'A wife isn't allowed to testify against her husband in a court of law,' she said with a shudder. 'Is that why you're marrying me?'

Preston drew a deep breath. 'Once we're married everything will be as it should have been between Ailsa and me.' He held up the tinkering music box. 'Wasn't this your way of letting me know you'd have my child?'

Saffron stared at him aghast. She had never wanted children. Being a mother wasn't in her DNA; she lacked the necessary maternal feelings required to make a success of motherhood.

'You've done nothing but lie to me ever since Ailsa's murder,' said Saffron, recoiling from him. 'How was I supposed to know you'd want a child?'

'For God's sake, you sound as sanctimonious as Ailsa,' said Preston, pounding his fist against the chest of drawers. 'She used to taunt me in public by saying she'd never ruin her figure by having a baby. I got so sick of hearing her say it...'

A shaft of fear shot through Saffron as Preston flung the tinkering music box against the wall. It dropped to the floor, rolled halfway across the room and went on playing...

Preston turned to her with a fierce glazed look in his eyes. Surely her dream couldn't have come to this. Yet hadn't Ailsa warned her? More than one person had told her of Preston's violent temper. Only she hadn't wanted to believe them.

Preston snatched the pistol from Saffron's hand before her scrambled thoughts had time to react. She stared back at him down the muzzle of the pistol – white faced with shock and disbelief.

I'm Saffron – not Ailsa, she wanted to scream only her fear was too strong...

The tinkering music box died in mid-note...

Preston was about to kill her and there was nothing she could do to stop him. She closed her eyes in nervous dread and then opened them seconds later to see a hand darting over Preston's shoulder. The pistol was wrenched firmly from his grasp. Three police officers had dashed out of the adjoining room and surrounded him.

Saffron turned her head as footsteps rang out from behind her. She was stunned as Dr. Foster entered the room from the hallway. It came to her in a flash – the arguing voices and the music box had all been part of a ruse to get Preston to confess to Ailsa's murder...

After Preston had been arrested and taken away by the police, Saffron found herself alone with the doctor.

'Why have you taken so long to admit to being Ailsa's real husband?' she demanded.

'Because there are less fortunate people in

this world than us,' said David Foster coldly. 'People who need the best medicine money can buy. Then there are women like Pearl Constantine. They'll donate money for new hospital wings if the whim takes them. Usually, it's after they've made fools of themselves by developing the hots for arrogant, self-opinionated doctors like me. The hospital now has the money to build a new wing. There's no way it would have that money if my marriage to Ailsa had come to light before now. According to Mrs. Constantine and her elite circle of friends, the Ailsa Kennedys of this world are corrupt, homewrecking sluts.'

Saffron's memory stirred and she once again found herself on the staircase landing in the moments leading up to the murder. She now knew what she had been too foolish to realize at the time. Ailsa hadn't been speaking to a lover – she'd been speaking to Preston about her marriage to David Foster.

'Can't you just accept I'm a married woman and leave it at that? Divorcing my husband for you would lead to all sorts of complications that are best avoided for

everyone's sake. Honestly, you're as bad as any other man I've known. Totally indifferent to anyone else's feelings apart from your own. Darling, how many times do I have to tell you? My being married to another man doesn't change my feelings for you....?'

'Why did you marry Ailsa in the first place?' asked Saffron bewilderedly.

'Ailsa's work visa for England and Europe was about to expire,' replied Dr. Foster. 'She married me because becoming a British citizen would enable her to continue with her financially lucrative ballet career. The money she paid me went towards the medical research I was doing at the time. We were only lovers for a short while. Owing to her busy schedule we soon drifted apart. It came as a complete surprise when we met up again here in the Blue Mountains. I'd never once intimated to her that I was interested in coming to Australia. We were both anxious to keep quiet about the past, but somehow Preston found out.'

'Couldn't you have gone about trapping Preston some other way?' said Saffron coldly.

'Why did you have to push him over the edge like that?'

'The police have been watching him like a hawk ever since Ailsa died,' said Dr. Foster. 'There was a very good chance he hadn't been able to get rid of the murder weapon before he arrived at the Katoomba Sports Centre that night. After you accepted his offer of marriage, the police had to move quickly to prevent you from marrying a murderer – hence tonight's charade with the voices and the music box. It's time you return to Sydney and get on with your life...'

Saffron later had no recollection of leaving the house she had dreamed of sharing with Preston and beginning the long drive back to Sydney. She felt as if a stranger had taken possession of her body. All her hopes and dreams had come to nothing – and yet the pain she was expecting to overwhelm her was curiously absent.

I've spent my entire life wanting to be like Ailsa, she thought with a sense of detachment that surprised her. *The clothes, the house and Preston have all been snatched from my grasp.*

David Foster has ruined everything for me – and yet somehow it doesn't matter...

Saffron's mind was clear and coherent – her gaze fixed resolutely on the road. The storm had abated and the Eucalyptus-scented air smelt wonderfully fresh. She felt a curious sense of peace as the BMW's headlights shone like moonbeams on the road ahead of her. It was as if she had always known in the back of her mind that her dream of marrying Preston would never amount to anything. There was a certain peace and contentment in acceptance.

An image of Ailsa's smiling face appeared in front of the windscreen. Saffron brushed one of her cheeks and was surprised to find it was wet with tears. She had been crying without realizing it. Owing to the heavy rainfall a tree from higher up on the mountainside had become dislodged and fallen across the road. She braked and attempted to steer around the fallen tree but instead found herself skidding sideways...

For as long as Saffron could remember, Ailsa had always enjoyed getting the better of her. But now that was in the past. She no longer needed to validate her existence by comparing herself to Ailsa...

As the BMW speared through the guard rail, shooting out into the soft, velvety darkness of the night, which concealed the jagged ravine far below, Ailsa's laughter came back to haunt Saffron – like a file grating on glass...

Also by Jared Cade

Murder on London Underground

A Lyle Revel and Hermione Bradbury mystery - # 2

Peter Hamilton, London Underground's managing director, is horrified when his ex-wife is pushed under a train.

Following the murder of a second commuter, he receives a phone call from an organisation calling itself Vortex that is dedicated to preventing the privatization of the network. 'You were the intended victim at Baker Street... Next time you won't be so lucky...'

In desperation, Hamilton turns for help to Lyle Revel and Hermione Bradbury, a glamorous couple with a talent for solving murders.

But as the death toll rises, the terrorists release a runaway train on the network...

'A chilling thriller and a great read' – Louise Burfitt-Dons, author of the PI Karen Andersen series

Printed in Great Britain
by Amazon